Mocha

A Red Line Coffee Shop Mystery Novella

by D. B. McNicol

COPYRIGHT

---

1.   http://donnamcnicol.com/

Chapter One

nd so it begins...

A "No, I'm okay. Stop worrying. I know it's your job, but I'm fine. I'll call you tomorrow after the competition. Oh, and tell Stevie 'thanks'. If she hadn't encouraged me to sign up, well, she knows." She took a deep breath before continuing. "I never expected to be in the final round. The top prize award would sure help with my college expenses." Jodi listened to her brother for a minute before continuing. "I promise. I will call you as soon as they post the results. I'm the second one to perform and there are only six of us. We should know something by tomorrow night. Gotta run, Desiree is waiting for me. Luv ya!"

She slipped the phone into her pocket and grabbed two sodas out of the mini-fridge before heading down the hallway to her best friend's room. The sounds of hysterical screams interrupted her thoughts and sent her running. When she realized it was coming from the direction of her destination, she almost tripped over her feet as she rushed into the room. "Dizzy, what's—"

It was obvious what was wrong. Desiree's roommate, Cynthia Peabody, was sprawled on the floor and very obviously dead. Her face was covered in powdered sugar apparently from the half-empty donut box beside her. She took a step forward just in time to catch Desiree as she fell backward.

Earlier...

The eight-week combination music camp and competition was sponsored by Whisper Peak Institute of Music and was being held on the their campus. Contestants had been divided into six categories: vocal, strings, keyboard, percussion, brass, and woodwind. Jodi was in the vocal category and her new friend Desiree was in the percussion group. The top winner in each category would get a five-thousand dollar cash award. Once all six category winners were chosen, they competed for the grand prize of twenty-five thousand dollars.

The weeks had passed quickly, with their time divided between classes and rehearsals. Friends had been made and so had enemies, as so often happens in competitions.

"I can't believe we both made the final round!" Jodi Delgado, aka Gabby, turned to her new best friend, Desiree Hopkins, aka Dizzy, and pulled her into a hug. The duo was well-known around the campus and had been given the combined nickname of Gab-zzy by the other contestants. They'd only known each other for a few weeks, having met on registration day, but immediately connected. They knew they'd be lifelong friends.

And back again...

The girls sat on the floor outside Dizzy's room as the campus police and medical staff swarmed around them, in and out of the room, up and down the hallway. They watched as Cynthia's body was wheeled away on a squeaking gurney. Other students lined the hallway, sharing their thoughts in soft murmurs as they stared at and pointed to Desiree.

Jodi whispered. "Ignore them, Diz. They don't know anything."

Tears streaked Desiree's cheeks. "They all know we weren't really friends. She was just so... so..." A sob stopped further words.

"It doesn't matter what anyone thinks. I mean, it looks like an accident of some sort." She pulled a tissue out of her pocket and handed it to her friend.

"Really?" Desiree blew her nose and tucked the tissue into the sleeve of her sweatshirt. "What do you think happened?"

Growing up as the younger sister of a police officer, Jodi knew better than to make wild guesses. "They won't know anything until the coroner's report." She paused. "Or if they have to do an autopsy..."

"What does that mean? Why would they do an autopsy?" Desiree sniffed and pulled the tissue out to wipe her nose.

"Well, if the coroner decides there is foul play or maybe just can't determine the cause of death, then the body would be sent to the medical examiner for the autopsy."

"How do you know all this stuff?"

"My brother is a police officer back home in Jumpers Hole. We only have a coroner." She leaned in closer. "And he also owns the funeral parlor in town. AND..." she paused dramatically, "his last name is Alldone. Can you imagine a funeral parlor named Alldone's Funeral Home?" She stifled a giggle, but Desiree couldn't, a snort escaping her lips as she tried to hold back her laugh, eliciting more stares and whispering from the others.

They were silenced by the sight of the two officers striding down the hallway with Wesley Sherman, the head of the music school. The trio stopped in front of the two girls.

"You were the ones who found the body?" The taller of the two officers asked in a brusque tone.

The girls nodded.

He continued. "We need to interview you." Turning to the Wesley he asked, "Is there a private room?"

Wesley blanched as he stammered, "Um, yes, no, um, certainly."

"We will need it after we examine the room. No one can enter until we release it. The crime scene techs should be here shortly." He turned to his partner, who nodded.

Wesley cleared his throat. "Please stand up, girls. I expect you to cooperate fully with the officers."

"Um, sir, will the competition be delayed?" Desiree asked.

"I hadn't—" He cleared his throat again. "Most certainly. We will hold an assembly to make the announcement."

Jodi chimed in, "It won't have to be cancelled, will it?"

Wesley looked at the officers and was met with two stone faces. "I'm not sure. I don't think so. I will need to talk to the board." He tugged on his ear, something he did when he was nervous. "I'd better go and call them now. May I?" He waited for one of the officers to nod.

The second officer mumbled something to the first, who then turned to the girls. "Officer Standish will take your information. You aren't to leave the campus until we interview you. Is that understood?"

They nodded as he turned to enter the room, his partner pulled out a pen and notebook. "Your names?"

Chapter Two

As she waited to talk to the police, Jodi let her memories flow. She had been so eager to leave when she drove off, excited even after a sleepless night full of hopes and dreams.

She had refused to look in the rear-view mirror as she drove away. Two months, that's all. Just two months of camp and she'd be back. Why did everyone make such a big deal out of her leaving? She slipped a glance in the mirror and saw her brother standing in the street, arms crossed, looking every bit the police official he was. Stephanie, aka Stevie, stood beside him, waving. Leathers and Alexandria had already turned back and were walking into the Red Line Coffee Shop.

The Red Line Coffee Shop was owned by Stevie and two other firefighters, Brett and Garrett. Leathers was the ever-present jack-of-all-trades who worked security at night and general handyman duties the rest of the time. He and Alexandria were an almost-couple, where you saw one, you'd see the other.

She let out a sigh. Eight weeks. Two months. It wasn't like she'd never been away from home. Well, maybe it was. But it was just a camp. A camp and a competition. An important competition. She'd love to win it, but doubted she had a chance. It was worth going just for the extra training and practice.

Stevie had been the one to talk her brother into paying for the event. Stevie had been married to her brother, Jay. Even though they were divorced, they maintained a close friendship.

She laughed, thinking about the conversation at the coffee shop the night before. Her brother had wanted to drive her and Stevie had called him on it, labeling him an overbearing big brother. He countered with the argument he just wanted to keep her safe. She and Stevie won in the end.

5

They were family, not by blood, but by love.

Looking back now, she sighed. The coffee shop had become a second home to her, a place where everyone treated her like family. She felt warm and safe there. Why had she left? The first day at music camp had been an eye-opener. She felt out of place, a small-town girl with all these other talented musicians. A goldfish swimming with sharks.

It wasn't long before she realized they were all the same, no matter their talent or background. She'd made friends, but now she was involved in the suspicious death of another competitor. Should she have left home?

☕

The official announcement had been made. The competitions were temporarily cancelled. If the police allowed, they would resume on Monday. The contestants studied the note on the bulletin board and the comments echoed in the hallway.

"Good thing it's almost the weekend."

"That's harsh. Someone died."

"I just wish we could leave the campus. I need some retail therapy."

"Retail therapy! Now that sounds like a plan."

"What's up?"

"No competitions until Monday."

"No practice sessions either."

"Anyone wanna go to town with me?"

"We can't leave the campus."

"You're kidding me!"

"Police orders."

"Did they interview you?"

"Not yet. I heard they spent hours talking to her roommate."

"You mean Dizzy?"

"Yeah."

"You think she did it?"

"Did what?"

"Killed Cyndi!"

"Why would she do that?"

"I heard they hated each other."

"Huh, I knew they weren't besties, but I'd suspect River first."

"River? Why?"

A shrug was the response.

"Really? River is one of the quietest girls here."

"You know you have to watch out for the quiet ones."

"I heard Cynthia was sweet on her, but River turned her down."

"What? Cyndi is, um, was gay? I had no idea."

"Me neither, but that's the rumor."

"Maybe you shouldn't spread rumors about the dead. Bad karma."

Snickers floated through the crowd, but were quickly shushed when Gabby and Dizzy approached. Nervous looks were exchanged as everyone moved aside to let the duo move to the bulletin board.

"Well, Diz, looks like we got the weekend off. Wanna go swimming?"

Desiree pasted a forced smile on her face. "Why not, Gabs, since they won't let anyone practice."

They turned back to the group, still standing silently, observing them. "Anyone else up for swimming?"

☕

They never made it to the pool. Ermine Elmore, school counselor and Wesley's assistant, stopped them in the hallway.

"Ladies. You need to be available for police interviews today."

"Um, we were just going swimming," Desiree responded.

"No, that won't work. It could be as early as the next hour."

Jodi frowned. "They couldn't give you an exact time?"

"I'm afraid not. They just requested you both remain available today."

"And we can't be available in the pool?" Jodi countered.

"That would be highly inappropriate. I don't think talking to the police while in bathing suits presents the school in a good light."

The girls exchanged looks and sighed.

"I suggest you wait in either the cafeteria or the library where you can be easily located."

"Cafeteria it is, right Gabs?"

"Works for me."

"Thank you, Ms. Elmore," they replied simultaneously.

She nodded and waddled away, mumbling about students and inappropriate behavior, leaving the duo giggling as they linked arms.

The cafeteria was almost empty. River Lawson sat at a table in the corner, her back to the room. A couple of school employees were at another table.

"Should we join her?" Desiree asked Gabby.

"Sure. Well, if she doesn't mind. She seems to keep to herself most of the time."

Desiree chuckled. "Even introverts need friends."

"Like you'd know anything about being introverted."

"Hey, don't call the kettle black!"

After picking up their drinks and some snacks, they approached the solo girl.

"Hey River. Do you mind if we sit?" Desiree asked.

She sighed and shrugged. "Suit yourself." She went back to reading her book.

"Thanks."

Desiree whispered to Jodi, "What do you think the police interview will be like?"

"No clue. I never watch police shows or read mystery books. Give me a good romance any day."

Desiree whispered back, "Isn't your brother a cop?"

"Yeah, but we never really talk about this kind of stuff."

River fidgeted in her seat as they continued to whisper back and forth. She finally slammed her book shut and announced, "I can tell you what it's like. It sucks!"

Jodi grimaced. "I'm sorry. We didn't mean to disturb you."

"What can you tell us?" Desiree asked. "They're going to talk to us today some time. Ms. Elmore wouldn't even let us go to the pool" She made a face and mimicked the conversation. "I don't think talking to the police while in bathing suits presents the school in a good light."

River couldn't help but laugh. "You sounded just like her."

"Have they talked to you yet, River?" Gabby asked.

"No, but I heard they are going to interrogate everyone before Monday."

Desiree inhaled sharply. "Interrogate? That sounds ominous. I thought it was more of an informal interview thing."

"Interview, interrogate - they're just words," River countered.

"I guess Gabs and I are first because we found the body." Desiree shivered.

"Did you really faint?"

"She did! She was lucky I was standing behind her and caught her or she might be dead, too."

River's eyes opened wide. "Really?"

"Um, no! I wouldn't have died."

"You could have had a concussion. Then you could have had a brain bleed."

"Stop being so dramatic, Gabs." Desiree grinned and River laughed.

The loudspeaker crackled and Ermine Elmore's voice boomed out, "Desiree Martinez to the conference room. Desiree Martinez. Please proceed to the conference room immediately."

Desiree stood. "Guess she means me. I'll see you when I see you!"

Chapter Three

❝ Please have a seat, Ms. Martinez. I'm Officer Richards and this is Officer Standish. We will be recording this conversation."

Desiree sat and under the table she intertwined her fingers to stop the shaking. "Do you know what happened to Cyndi?" She took a deep breath, realizing her voice was trembling.

"I'm sorry, but we can't divulge any information at this point in the investigation."

"Oh, okay. Sorry."

Officer Standish smiled. "No worries. We just need to ask you a few questions about what you saw when you entered the room and found your roommate's body."

"Um, I did tell you that yesterday."

"Yes, but there may be things you forgot to mention or that will come to mind during this interview."

"Okay, I see. Do I just talk or do you ask questions?"

Officer Richards frowned and cleared his throat, taking control of the conversation back. "We will be asking the questions. I'm going to start the interview." He clicked the recorder and stated the date, the names of those present, and the case number. "Desiree Martinez, you are attending the music camp and competition at Whisper Peak Institute of Music and Cynthia Peabody was your roommate. Is that correct?"

Desiree nodded.

"Please reply out loud," Officer Richards chided.

"Yes, sir."

"Cynthia Peabody was your roommate?"

"Yes, sir."

"You were friends?"

"More like friendly. We were competitors. Yeah, friendly competitors."

"Did you ever argue?"

Desiree thought before shaking her head. "Not that I can remember. We didn't really interact all that much."

"What do you mean?"

"We were in different groups. I'm in the percussion group and she is, um, was in the keyboards group." Getting no response from the officer, she further explained, "She played piano and I play drums. Most of our rehearsals till last week were in our own groups. Once we were selected as finalists in our own groups, then we started working together as a band."

Officer Standish asked, "Didn't you see each other every night and morning?"

"Not really. She was an early bird and got up at sunrise for yoga. Me? I like my sleep and could stay up till all hours. So no, we didn't see each other all that much."

Officer Richards spoke next. "Please describe your typical day for us, starting with your arrival here on campus."

"Well, the first two weeks were spent with the mornings in classes for our musical groups and the afternoons in rehearsals. The next two weeks were morning classes and afternoon competitions without elimination. By week five, we had the mornings off and the afternoon competitions were with eliminations. Last week, week six, the finalists were announced. Then we started rehearsing as a band."

Office Standish held up his hand and asked, "So you weren't in direct competition with the victim until this week?"

"Actually, this week was just rehearsals. Next week we would be starting the final competitions. Each of us would have a solo, a duet or trio, and a band set to perform. At the end there would be one final winner. That person would be awarded the grand prize scholarship."

"And that was a significant prize?" Officer Richards asked.

"Yes. Twenty-five thousand dollars."

Officer Standish whistled, and Officer Richards frowned at him before continuing. "What about the donuts scattered in your room? Was the victim a big sweet eater?"

"Not really. But Gabby, um, Jodi Delgado, and I had sort of a routine. She would pick up mocha coffees from the coffee truck, and I'd get a dozen donuts from the food truck. We'd bring them to the group rehearsals with us. We started with them just for us—"

"Why?"

"Well, we sort of clicked and became friends the first day when we bumped into each other... I mean literally, bumped into each other. She'd get two mochas, I'd get two donuts and that would be our breakfast before classes. When we both made it to the finals, we picked them up for all six of us."

"The six being..."

She sighed. "Me, Jodi Delgado, River Lawson, Jonathan Coleman, Tyler Hawkins, and Cynthia Peabody."

"And everyone ate the donuts and drank the coffees?"

"Sure, why not? I mean, they didn't pay for them. We did."

"Why was that?"

"It was Gabby, um, Jodi's idea. Sort of a goodwill gesture. She said that even though there could only be one winner, we were all in it together and we were all winners. Plus, we had no idea of the financial situation of the others, so it was easy this way."

"Were you trying to bribe the others in any way?"

She snorted. "You're not serious, are you?" One look at his face told her he was, in fact, very serious. "No, there was no intent to bribe anyone, in any way. We are all serious musicians. This has been an important time for us. We all plan careers in music. And if we were going to bribe anyone, wouldn't it be the staff who were judging us?"

Changing the subject, he continued, "What did you see when you entered your room yesterday?"

"Cynthia on the floor, all pale and grayish."

"That was all you noticed?"

"Well, she had powdered sugar all over her lips and a half-eaten donut in her hand. Oh, and there was an open box of donuts on the desk."

"Your desk?"

"Um, our desk. We shared it."

With no change in expression, Officer Richards continued. "Did you deliver the box of donuts to your room yesterday?"

"No!"

"The day before?"

"No!"

"Do you know who did?"

"No!" She crossed her arms and glared at him. Before he could ask another question, she bolted straight up in her seat, leaned forward, and demanded, "Did the donuts kill her?"

He stood and motioned for Officer Standish to open the door. "Thank you for your time. Please do not leave the campus. We may need to ask you some further questions. And do not, under any circumstances, discuss the details of this interview with anyone outside this room. Understand?"

"Sure. Fine. Whatever." She stormed out of the room but stopped when Officer Richards called out to her.

"Please ask Ms. Delgado to come to the conference room next."

Chapter Four

J odi continued her video call with the plea, "Please, Stevie. Don't tell Jay or he'll drive up here and try to butt into the investigation."

"You're right about that. But are you sure you should stay?"

"I have to, at least until they release us."

"Have they said what killed her?"

"No. It could have been a heart attack for all we know. The donuts might be totally incidental. Cyndi was a real type-A personality. She might have just cracked and wanted a sugar binge."

Stevie laughed. "You could be right. I just wish they'd figure it out. At least you or your friend aren't suspects."

"Well, not yet. Dizzy still worries about the donut angle, and she won't stop until they tell us how Cyndi did die."

"How many more interviews are there?"

"I think one, maybe two more. I haven't talked with the others."

"Why is that?"

"They won't allow us to talk about it until they are done with their investigation. The only reason Diz and I can still talk is cause we found the body together. And she's my new roomie since mine left after her elimination."

"Can I tell anyone else? Like maybe Garrett and Brett? Or Leathers?"

"Please no. Well, Leathers maybe. He knows how to keep things to himself. I guess you want to be able to bounce this off someone else."

"I do. We helped Garrett out of his mess, maybe we can figure out a way to help you."

"I'm not IN a mess. At least not yet. If anyone is, it's Dizzy. You'd like her. She's a lot like you."

"Oh? In what way?"

"Outspoken, adventurous, resourceful, and kind. Just don't cross her."

Stevie laughed. "Okay, I see what you mean. Please keep me updated as much as possible. I'm ready to help any way I can."

"Thanks, Stevie. Just talking to you helps. Ciao!"

"Later, gator!"

The call clicked off and Jodi lay back on her bed, replaying her interview with the police. They had asked her all the general questions she expected. How did she know the victim? Were they friends? Did she know if Desiree and the victim had been having any disagreements or arguments? Did she know anyone who might have had issues with the victim? What was her daily routine?

She and Desiree had compared notes afterwards. They both felt there were no surprises. Well, except the donut angle. That puzzled both of them.

The door opened, letting in the bright hallway light. "Ugh! Close the door, you're blinding me."

Desiree laughed. "You always have to be so dramatic!"

"What? Me? You're the dramatic one," Jodi countered. She plopped backwards on the other bed, propping her feet up against the wall. "You finish your call home?"

"Yup. Not much news there."

"How did your friend react? She's kinda your ex-sister-in-law, right?"

Jodi nodded. "And she got me the job at the Red Line Coffee Shop, too. I don't know why she and my brother broke up. I was too busy with high school. I'm glad they stayed friends."

"So, what did she have to say about my roomie and THE EVENT?"

"She was a bit stunned and more than ready to come and help. I told her there was no need. I made her promise not to tell my brother, though. There's no way he wouldn't show up and try to muscle into the investigation."

"Huh. Sounds like they both like to be in the middle of the action?"

"Yeah. Kinda explains their career choices in fire and police, doesn't it."

"Maybe that's why they split up? They were both controlling, action-oriented people?'

Jodi shrugged. "Like I said, I'm not sure. But that does make sense."

"What do you make of all this? I wish they would tell us how she died. I hate not knowing what's going on." Desiree flipped around and sat on the edge of the bed.

Jodi rolled onto her side and propped her head up on her elbow. "They didn't make a big deal of the donuts with me, just the coffee. Guess that's because I bought it." She bolted upright. "Hey! Did you notice a coffee cup from the coffee truck in your room when we found Cyndi?"

"Um, I kinda fainted, remember? I didn't see anything but the body on the floor."

"I wish we could get back into the room. We might find some clues that were missed."

"You don't think Frick and Frack were thorough? I mean, they did call in the crime scene techs."

"You'd be surprised what can be missed. Sometimes it's the most obvious things. Things that others wouldn't realize were important."

"Well, we can't. They have the room barricaded with crime scene tape."

"And yet, they haven't declared it a crime scene. At least, not officially." Jodi stroked her chin in an attempt to look mysterious, and Dizzy did the same, causing them both to collapse in laughter.

☕

Jodi shushed Desiree. "Stop giggling! Someone will hear us."

"I can't help it. I giggle when I'm nervous."

Turning to face her friend, Jodi frowned. "And why should you be nervous? This IS your room. You have every right to go in and get your stuff."

"Um, I don't think so. Not with crime scene tape across the door. We can look and take some pictures, but I'm not touching anything. And I'm darn sure not removing anything! I don't want to go to jail. Do you?"

Jodi snorted. "We're not going to jail. If we get caught, we just tell them you needed some of your feminine supplies. That always stops men in their tracks."

Desiree giggled again. "You are so right. We're almost there. Turn on your phone flashlight."

Jodi reached for her phone in her back pocket—

"STOP! What are you girls doing here?" Ermine Elmore demanded.

Jodi gulped. "Oh, Ms. Elmore. I'm sorry, we didn't mean to startle you."

"Yes, sorry, ma'am. I need to get some of my feminine products out of my room."

"Oh, no you don't! You are not to enter that room. You can visit the school nurse in the morning if you need something. Back to your room. NOW!" She waved her hand, shooing them back the way they came.

They raced back to Jodi's room and slammed the door behind them, laughing.

"I knew we'd get caught," Desiree muttered.

"Yeah, maybe. But you should never have tried the feminine products bit on another woman. Especially HER! And I wonder what she was doing there?"

"I know. That was strange. It's well after midnight. But then again, she is strange!"

"Enough adventure and speculation for today. Let's crash with some tunes and catch at least a couple hours of sleep. Then we can tackle this again."

Desiree yawned. "And maybe the police will have some answers. Like hopefully she died from natural causes." She clicked the remote for the radio. "Gabs? You still awake?" Hearing no response, she sighed and nestled into her bed. "Natural causes, that's it."

Chapter Five

E arly Saturday morning, shouting voices blasting through the open window woke both girls. Jodi sat up and groggily croaked, "What the heck is all that racket?"

Desiree mumbled, "It's too early. Need sleep."

"Diz, it's after ten. Get up! Something is going on."

"You go see what it is and come back to tell me. Need more sleep." She rolled over, turning her back to Jodi.

"Fine, but I'm not coming back, so you'll never know what you're missing." She knew Diz couldn't stand being out of the know.

"Darn you! You're gonna make me get up, aren't you?" She rolled over again and sat on the edge of the bed, rubbing her eyes. "Are you happy? You got me up."

Jodi grabbed her arm and tugged her up. "We slept in our clothes. We're fine. Let's go. Now!"

"Can't I brush my teeth? My mouth tastes like a garbage dump."

"Chew some gum! Let's go before everyone leaves and we have no idea what happened."

Desiree sighed, "One minute..." She ran her brush through her hair and pulled it into a ponytail. "You got some gum?"

"You make me so glad I got my hair cut this summer. Short is easy. Tousle it and I'm good to go."

"Um, gum?"

"No, I don't have any." She rummaged through her bag. "But I do have a couple of breath mints." She held them out.

"Why didn't you say so?" Diz grabbed them and tossed them in her mouth. Immediately, she sucked in a breath. "These are hot!"

"Wimp! Let's go."

They navigated using the voices like a compass and found themselves in the cafeteria, along with at least a dozen others. They spotted River at the edge of the group.

"Psst, River. What's all the commotion about?" Jodi asked.

"Jonathan overhead Mr. Sherman and Ms. Elmore talking about the investigation. They've declared Cynthia's death as murder. Can you believe it?"

"What the—! Murder? Did they say how they knew? How she died?"

River stared at Desiree. "She was poisoned!"

Desiree turned white and said more loudly than intended, "What?"

The crowd turned around, whispers raced from person to person along with suspicious stares at Desiree.

River nodded. "Serious as a broken cell phone!"

"Do they know how she was poisoned?" Jodi asked.

River shook her head. "That was all Jon overheard." She scanned the room, looking for him. When she saw him, she shouted his name and motioned for him to come over.

Jonathan never did anything in a hurry. He eventually sauntered over and asked, "What's up?"

"I was just telling Gab-zzy what you overheard this morning."

"Oh yeah, man. That's scary. Someone poisoned Cynthia. What's up with that?"

"You didn't hear anything else?" Jodi asked.

He shrugged. "Not really. Nothing about how or who or stuff. Just that it was considered foul play."

River shivered. "That's harsh. I guess we're all here until they find the killer?"

"S'pose so. Gotta run." Jonathan walked off.

Desiree grimaced. "Well, not sure I like the sounds of that. How long can they keep us here? Oh, wait! Does that mean one of US is a killer?"

"I don't think so, do you really? I mean, we're all dedicated to our music, but murder? And why would anyone here want to murder one of us? Makes no sense." Jodi shook her head. "Think about it. Means, motive, and opportunity. That's what they'll be looking for."

"The only motive I can think of would be to wipe out one contestant for the grand prize."

"And that makes no sense since I heard the runner-up in her grouping will be bumped up to the finals now."

"Okay, so motive is out. You said means and opportunity."

Jodi nodded.

"Means, that would be how she was killed. Right?"

Jodi nodded again.

"Got no guesses on that since we don't know what poison was used. So, opportunity. Still got nothing. How do the detectives on TV make it look so easy?"

Jodi laughed. "It's called fiction for a reason."

☕

The school administrator and his assistant entered the conference room and sat opposite the two officers. Officer Richards broke the news.

Wesley blanched and tugged his ear. "What do you mean, no one can go home until you complete your investigation?"

"Surely you don't mean the students?" Ermine interjected. "We have our final competition coming up and then they go home."

Officer Richards frowned. "I understand that, but until we have found out who was involved in the death of Ms. Peabody, they are all suspects."

"And that means no one leaves. Even you two," Office Standish added.

"Well, I..." Ermine grumbled. "Surely you don't suspect Mr. Sherman or me in the murder of a student. That is preposterous."

"As I said, everyone is a suspect until cleared. We need to set up new interviews with everyone on campus. And that includes anyone who was on campus the day the body was found, even if they are no longer located here. Officer Standish will remain to get the list and then will work with you to schedule the interviews." He stood and extended his hand, the meeting over.

"It will take me several hours to research the information you need, Officer Standish. You might be more comfortable waiting in the cafeteria?" Ermine stood and waited.

"Thank you. I'm fine here. I prefer not to mingle with the students until interview time."

"Can I bring you some coffee? A soft drink?" she asked.

"Coffee would be nice. Thank you."

"Cream or sugar?"

"Black, please."

Ermine nodded and left the room, returning with a cup and a carafe of coffee.

He poured out a cup and took a sip. "Thank you. This is excellent coffee."

Ermine beamed. "We pride ourselves on using top-grade food goods. Many of the products are locally sourced."

"Really, interesting. I'd like a list of all your food vendors as well as the other list."

She sighed. "Certainly. Anything else I can get you?"

"No, thank you. I'm good."

Ermine left the room muttering something about uppity public servants, leaving a chuckling officer behind.

Chapter Six

One by one, the police called in staff members, vendors, contestants and anyone else who was on campus the day of the murder. They still hadn't released any news publicly about what poison was found in Cynthia's body, causing rumors to fly around the campus like butterflies on a spring day.

Wesley had determined the rehearsals for the final competition would resume since no one could leave for home, including the previously eliminated contestants. By Monday morning, the anticipation for Wesley's announcement had reached fever pitch. Everyone gathered in the auditorium and waited for his appearance, whispers ricocheting into echoes.

Desiree leaned closer to Jodi. "Do you think he's going to tell us more about Cyndi?"

"I don't know. Probably not since the police still aren't done with the interviews. My appointment is at two this afternoon. You?"

"Four o'clock today. I'm not sure what else I can tell them."

"Me neither, but maybe we can get them to share something about what they've found out."

"You think?"

Jodi snorted. "Not really. We'll probably be the last to know. Shhh, Mr. Sherman just walked in."

Tapping the microphone to check if it was on, Wesley cleared his throat. "Thank you all for coming today. I know it's been several days of uncertainty, but we're back on track now. The death of a student will never be taken lightly, but I'm sure Ms. Peabody would want us to continue on, even as the police continue their interview process. I know you will all cooperate fully. In the meantime, we have selected the runner-up in the piano category to replace Ms. Peabody. Amelia Hancock, please stand. Please join me in giving her some applause for stepping in and allowing us to continue the competition."

Someone in the back of the room shouted, "Maybe she took out her competition!"

Amelia immediately sat back down.

Wesley bristled. "We'll have none of those types of accusations or speculations. Let the police do their job and you do yours."

Another voice shouted, "When do we start?"

"Thank you. Individual rehearsals will commence today. Group rehearsals will remain on hold until the police have concluded all their interviews."

"When will that be?"

"I believe today is the final grouping of interviews. Watch the bulletin board for any updates on the resumption of the group rehearsal. In the meantime, you should all contact your families and update them on the delay. Ms. Elmore, do you have anything to contribute?"

Ermine moved to the microphone. "Just that all rumors should be squashed immediately. They help no one and can actually hurt some. Thank you." She stepped back and nodded to Wesley.

"Good words for us all to practice. Thank you, Ms. Elmore. You all have the rest of the morning to prepare for your individual rehearsal time this afternoon. Your rehearsal schedule is now posted on the bulletin board. Please respect the other contestants and be on time. Again, thank you for your patience and cooperation."

"I wonder who else is left to be interviewed besides us?" Desiree whispered to Jodi.

"No idea. Let's just concentrate on our solo rehearsals. Are you ready?"

Desiree retorted. "I'm always ready." She beat rhythmically on her legs. "See?"

Jodi laughed. "You're such a goof sometimes."

"And that's why you love me. Let's hit the coffee and donut truck."

"Sounds good to me."

☕

Jodi spread a blanket under the big oak tree so they could sit and enjoy their snack.

"I think this is my favorite spot on campus. Arizona doesn't have trees like this." Desiree leaned back on the tree and sipped her coffee.

"I thought you lived here. I didn't realize they allowed competitors from outside the state."

"I lived in Arizona until college, then I moved here. The northeast is so different, but for some reason it feels like home. Even after only being here a couple of years."

"Is your family still in Arizona?"

"Only my older brother. Our parents died in a car crash two years ago."

"Dang! That's so sad." Jodi took a bit of her donut. "These things are addictive. I wonder what they put in them." She wiped her mouth and continued. "We never talked much about personal stuff, just silly things. I'm sorry about that. I should have known something was up when I mentioned my brother was a cop and the conversation switched to another topic."

"Don't worry about it. We just hit it off so quickly, we never really talked about our lives."

Jodi's cell phone buzzed, and she answered. "Gabby Delgado, at your service," causing Desiree to giggle. "Oh hi, Stevie." *pause* "No, nothing new. We are starting back on rehearsals though." *pause* "Yeah, that's a good thing." *pause* "I promise to let you know if we learn anything new. Jay still in the dark?" *pause* "Great, thanks. I'll call you when we know something. Bye."

"Your boss?"

Jodi nodded and took another bite of her donut, following it with a sip of coffee. "You heard my side of the conversation. Not much to tell her, but at least she's kept my brother from knowing."

"So, you wanna trade facts?"

"Sure. You want to start?"

"Okay. I'm twenty-one, orphaned, with one older brother. I've played the drums since I was about three or four. I lived in Arizona all my life until college when I moved here. I love most all foods except spinach. Rock and blues are my favorite music jams. Oh, and I'm addicted to chocolate and jelly-filled donuts. You?"

"Well, I've lived in the same town all my life. I'm twenty-one, too, and have an older brother, but my parents are still alive. They moved to Florida when I started college, they're both retired. I'm not a fan of any vegetables, but I'll never pass on a good burger. My music taste is all over the place, but for singing I do love the blues. So much emotion."

"Well, that about covers it. Let's get serious." Desiree put on a serious face. "Who do YOU think killed Cyndi, and why?"

"I really have no clue. It's still hard to believe someone would kill one of us. I know she was a bit standoffish, and everyone thought she felt she was better than all of us. But murder? Gives me the shivers."

"Well, at least we know it wasn't you or me!"

"Do we?" Jodi wiggled her eyebrows, and they both convulsed with laughter.

Chapter Seven

Officers Mitchell Richards and Trent Standish sat in a corner of the school cafeteria, mulling over the most recent interviews while they ate lunch.

Trent wiped a spot of mayonnaise off his mouth. "I really don't see where we're getting anywhere with this. Seems like a waste of time. These kids aren't involved."

Being the senior officer, Mitchell disagreed. "You never know where you might find a clue. Even with kids."

Trent shrugged. "I guess you're right. And they are all eighteen or over, so not really kids."

"Then factor in motive. These final contestants had the most motive since they are all competing for the same grand prize." He took a breath in, held it, then intoned in a deep voice, "There can be only one..." Trent stared at him "What? You don't get it?"

"Nope." He took another bite of his sandwich."

"The movie *Highlander*?"

"Never heard of it."

"You've led a deprived life."

Trent stood as Mitchell shook his head in disbelief. "Ready for the next one?"

Mitchell looked at his watch. "We've got another fifteen minutes. Sit down and relax."

Trent sat and impatiently tapped his foot.

"What's up with you today? You seem extra antsy."

"It's Big Betty. She's got a big birthday coming and as the unofficial matriarch in the house, I need to be sure it's extra special."

"She raised you and your baby sister after your parents passed, right?"

"Yeah. She put up with a lot from us. Well, mostly me. I wasn't a fun teenager to raise."

"How old will she be?"

Trent counted quietly before replying, "Fifty."

"Ah, the big five-o. Yup, that's a special one. Who are you inviting?"

"She's been a foster mom to so many, and I've sent invites to them all. Almost eighty percent have responded with a yes."

Mitchell grinned. "And that is how many?"

"Um, twenty-eight, I think. Then another dozen or so locals that have known her for years, her best friend, and my sister."

"So you're looking at maybe fifty folks?"

Trent counted quietly again. "Yeah, that sounds right. I have no idea where to hold it. That's the first thing I have to resolve."

"When is it?"

Trent sighed. 'Two weeks. Now you see why I want to get this wrapped up. I need to get my head into the planning, not playing around with these kids."

Mitchell cleared his throat. "You do remember this is a murder investigation, don't you?"

"I know, it's just—"

"No buts. It's our job to find the killer and put them behind bars so the justice system can do their work. And until that's done, Big Betty's party is on the back burner. Capiche?" He looked at his watch. "Time to go. Grab your stuff and we'll drop it in the trash on the way to the conference room."

☕

Two o'clock on the dot, and Jodi entered the conference room for her interview. She was determined she wouldn't let the officers bully her, and she would get as much new information from them as she could.

Officer Richards motioned for her to sit. "Thank you for joining us again. We don't plan to take up a lot of your time, just need to clarify a few things."

She smiled and waited.

He continued. "How well did you know the deceased?"

"Well, we were in different groups since she was piano and I'm vocals, so not real well. Sort of a 'Hi, how are you?' basis."

"But you were good friends with her roommate. Is that correct?"

She glared back. "Yes. Desiree and I have become good friends. She's rooming with me now since she can't get into her room."

Officer Standish smiled. "Hopefully she will get access to her room soon. Sorry about that."

She shrugged as Office Richards continued. "What do you know of the relationship between Ms. Martinez and Ms. Peabody?"

"Not much. Cynthia, Ms. Peabody, kept to herself mostly."

"Why was that?"

"Not sure, kind of like maybe she thought she was better than the rest of us."

"Oh?"

"Or maybe she was just an introvert. Most of us are extroverts and love to talk. Like I said, she mostly kept to herself."

"I understand during the last two weeks the six finalists have been to the same rehearsals."

She nodded.

"And you brought coffee for all six every morning."

She nodded again.

"And Ms. Martinez brought donuts for all six every morning."

"Yes, six mochas from me and a dozen mixed donuts from Dizzy, um, Desiree."

"And whose idea was that?"

She thought for a moment. "I'm not sure, it just sort of developed. We did it just for us in the early weeks. We both like our sleep and never had time to get breakfast in the cafeteria with the others. So coffee and donuts became our ritual."

"You said mocha coffees, right?"

"Yes."

"And mixed donuts?"

"Most times. It depended on what was available on the truck."

"Truck?"

"The food truck, the one with the donuts. They're in the parking lot every morning with a couple more around lunchtime and dinnertime. Guess not everyone wanted cafeteria food."

"What was the name of that truck?"

"The coffee truck was Cool Beans. The donut truck was..." She thought for a minute, snapped her fingers and added, "Rolling Dough."

"Do you know if the deceased frequented these trucks?"

"Who knows? Like I said, she kept to herself."

"Did she partake of the coffee and donuts you and Ms. Martinez provided?"

"As best as I can remember, yes. The other four in the finals all enjoyed them."

"On the day you found Ms. Peabody, did you see the box of donuts in her room?"

"I vaguely remember seeing an open box. And she appeared to have powdered sugar on her face, maybe from the donuts. Wait, were the donuts poisoned?"

Ignoring her question, he continued. "Did Ms. Martinez provide that box of donuts?"

"I don't think so. It was late in the day and I was on my way to meet up with Dizzy, Ms. Martinez."

"And you met her where?"

"Well, we had just left our afternoon solo rehearsals. We did the group in the mornings. She was going to her room for a sweatshirt, and I was grabbing a couple of sodas out of my mini-fridge. I remember I was talking to my brother—" She cleared her throat, "Officer Jay Delgado back home. I hung up, grabbed the sodas and as I left my room, I heard Dizzy scream. I got there seconds later and caught her as she fainted."

"She had just gotten to her room?"

"As far as I know. I wasn't actually there when she arrived."

"But she had been with you all afternoon?"

"Well, not WITH me, but in rehearsal."

"So, no one was with her?"

"She was in the studio. One of the sound techs might have been in there. They popped in and out, helping us as needed."

"Do you know if she purchased a box of donuts and left them in her room?"

Gabby paused, realizing she had no idea who had purchased the donuts. "Um, no, I don't know who bought them or brought them to the room."

Officer Richards stood. "Thank you. Please remember to keep this interview private. You are not to discuss anything you've said or heard here with anyone else."

Officer Standish added, "Especially with Ms. Martinez."

"And why is that? Do you really think she killed Cyndi? I mean, c'mon. You can't suspect her. I know she had a motive. Heck, we all did. And opportunity—" She stopped and whispered under her breath, "and means." She stared at the two officers standing in front of her like two statues. "Okay. I won't say anything. But I still can't believe it. No, not Dizzy." She walked out shaking her head.

Chapter Eight

J odi returned to the cafeteria and spotted several of the finalists seated at a table. As she approached, River called out. "Come sit. Your interview done?"

"Yes, and I hate this. All these suspicions and no facts."

"What did they ask you?" Tyler Hawkins joined in.

She made a motion zipping her mouth shut. "Can't discuss it."

"That sucks. Mine is at five. I just want to get it over with." River grimaced and asked Jonathan, "When is yours?"

"Done and done at one. Easy-peasy. But yeah, like Gabby, I can't discuss it."

"Dizzy is at four. Who else hasn't done theirs yet? Amelia?" Jodi asked.

"I was noon, so I'm done."

"Tyler?"

He looked at his watch. "I'm at three, so I've still got a little time. Any trick questions?"

Jodi snorted. "Not unless you killed Cyndi." The group exchanged awkward glances. Looking around the room she asked, "Anyone know where Dizzy is? I thought she'd be here." Getting no response, she stood. "Guess I'd better go find her. Later!"

Back in the room she now shared with her friend, there was no sign of Desiree. *I wonder where she is?* She tried calling her cell, but it went immediately to voicemail. She snapped her fingers as she remembered, "Solo rehearsal, duh!" She laughed as she grabbed a soda and headed back to the cafeteria.

"We need to check out the food trucks again. I really don't think the roommate did it. The timeline just doesn't hold up." Trent took a sip of his coffee.

"Maybe. But we know the poison was in all the donuts, eaten or not." Mitchell chuckled. "Sorry. All this talk of donuts makes me want some."

"I know what you mean. But we still need to find out who did purchase them and bring them into the room. But no one is confessing to buying them — yet."

They sat quietly for a moment, then Trent sat upright. "You do realize that maybe she wasn't the intended victim? Desiree Martinez bought donuts every day and everyone knew what she liked. Maybe she was the intended victim."

"Good work, Standish. I hate to admit it, but that thought never occurred to me. We might present that to her when she gets here. Who would have wanted to see her dead, that sort of thing."

"Hey, we should never block out any theories. Right?"

"Right."

Just then, Desiree popped her head in. "Are you ready for me?"

"Please, sit down." Officer Standish motioned to the chair opposite the officers.

"Will this take long? I need to meet up with some friends for dinner." She smiled and added, "That's assuming we can leave campus now that we've all been re-interviewed?"

"I'm afraid not."

She sighed. "Soon maybe? This cafeteria food is getting old."

Officer Richards cleared his throat. "It's really for everyone's safety. It's not a punishment."

"Fine. I guess I understand." She straightened up and wiggled in the uncomfortable chair. "I don't suppose we could order delivery? Or is that against the rules, too?"

"That could be worked out. We will give the administrator a list of places you can order from, ones that we have cleared."

"Uh, before dinner maybe?"

Officer Standish laughed. "I will get it to them before we leave today."

"Thank you. So, what are my questions?"

The two officers exchanged glances, and Officer Richards spoke first. "Could you please recount your activities and whereabouts on the day you discovered the body of Ms. Peabody?"

Desiree went into minute detail of her day, ending with her fainting into Jodi's arms.

"Not a great end to the day." She shook her head as she pictured the corpse in her room.

"Can you think of anyone who might have wanted Ms. Peabody dead?"

"No. She was pretty introverted, although some folks thought she was just a snob. She was very professional while here and very devoted to her craft."

"Did she ever mention a boyfriend or an ex?"

Desiree sighed. "I have to admit, we never really chatted about personal stuff. I don't even know where she was from, never mind any personal relationships. Sorry, no help here."

Mitchell nodded to Trent who took over the questioning. "Can you think of anyone who might want to hurt you or see you dead?"

"What?" Desiree's eyes widened. "Surely you don't—" She looked from one officer to the other. "Me? Are you serious?"

"It did occur to us that maybe Ms. Peabody wasn't the intended target. The donuts may have been delivered to your room with the intent you would indulge."

"I can't— It doesn't— I just—" Desiree stammered and closed her eyes before continuing. "I can't think of anyone who... I mean, it just makes no sense"

"Stranger things have happened. So, can you think of anyone with a reason to want to harm you?"

"No! I mean, I'm orphaned. My brother lives in Arizona and he's a youth counselor."

"Could he have gotten involved in drugs somehow?"

"NO! That's what he fights against."

"Maybe they sent someone after you to pressure him?"

"No, again. Besides, no one but him even knows where I am, where I moved to."

"Well, we have to consider all alternatives. We will need your brother's contact information."

Desiree crossed her arms and leaned back in the chair. "Fine, but you're wrong."

Trent shrugged. "Maybe, maybe not. In the meantime, you are all still quarantined here on campus."

"Argh!"

"It's for your protection."

"Fine. Anything else?"

"Just a few more questions. You said you bought donuts every morning. Was that from the..." he paused and looked at his notes, "The Rolling Dough food truck."

She nodded.

"Did the same person wait on you every day?"

She paused and thought. "Initially, it was the owner, I think. Um. Roberta was her first name. It was on her name tag. Then a younger man took over. He didn't wear a tag and wasn't uber-friendly so no idea what his name was."

"Did the owner return?"

"Not yet, that I know of. Just the same guy."

"Can you describe him?"

"Um, twenty-something, sandy hair cut really short. Maybe five-foot-ten-ish and close to two hundred pounds. He seemed very intense. Oh, and really light blue eyes. Maybe contacts?"

"Thank you. We did interview all the truck vendors, but I don't think we met with him. Must have been the owner, Roberta, you spoke of."

She sighed. "Is that all? Should I call my brother and let him know to expect a call from you?"

"We'd prefer not. Let us make the contact. When was the last time you talked to him?"

"When I moved onto the campus for the competition. I told him I didn't need the distractions. He can be a bit over-bearing." Under her breath she muttered, "Typical older brother."

"Thank you for your time, Ms. Martinez. We will be in touch. Please let us know if you think of anything else."

"Yeah, can I go—"

She was interrupted by the sound of an ear-splitting fire alarm.

Chapter Nine

T he cafeteria erupted into a state of chaos. River, Jonathan, Amelia, and Jodi jumped up and raced to the windows.

"Probably just a drill."

"Where's the fire?"

"Should we go wait outside?"

"Do you see smoke?"

"It'll be a false alarm."

"Do we have to leave?"

The loudspeaker crackled, and Wesley Sherman's voice boomed out. "Please evacuate all the buildings immediately. This is not a drill. I repeat, please leave all buildings on campus. Thank you."

"Guess that means us. Let's go," Jonathan prompted.

"I wonder where the fire is?" Amelia asked as they headed outdoors.

Gabby looked around. "Where's Tyler?"

"He had a headache and went to take a nap," River responded.

"I hope the alarm wakes him." Amelia joined in.

The parking lot was filled with summer students in other programs, as well as the school staff. Everyone milled around waiting for the all-clear announcement so they could return to their rooms.

Desiree approached her friends with the two officers in tow. Mitchell and Trent continued on towards the administration building as two fire trucks and an ambulance approached at a breakneck speed.

"What's up, guys?" she asked.

"No idea. How'd your interview go? Did you get the 'DON'T TALK ABOUT IT' warning?"

"Nope, so I guess I can talk."

Jodi snickered, "Like that's ever been a problem."

Desiree elbowed her. "Okay pot, quit calling the kettle black."

Jodi pulled her away from the others. "So spill. What did they have to say?"

"They think I might have been the target instead of Cyndi. Can you believe that? They told me I had to stay on campus for my protection. We all do."

"Yeah, they hinted at that with me, too, but I couldn't believe it. Why you?"

Desiree shrugged. "Not a clue. They even suggested it might have something to do with my brother. I told them that was nuts."

"The whole thing just gets stranger and—"

The ambulance crew emerged from the dormitory building with someone on the stretcher. People in the crowd started shouting to the others.

"Hey look, they're bringing out a body!"

"Who is it?"

"I don't know, I can't see—"

"That's Tyler!" River shrieked. "They're taking Tyler away in the ambulance!"

☕

"Why can't we go visit Tyler? He's our friend," Jonathan demanded an answer from the officers.

Hands on her hips, River put on her fiercest face. "Yeah, he needs our support."

Officer Richards scowled. "As we have previously and repeatedly stated, it isn't safe for any of you to leave the campus. We will be interviewing your friend this afternoon. According to the reports we've received, he could be returning as soon as tomorrow."

Officer Standish added, "That's the best we can do. So please, let us continue our work and you continue your rehearsals."

"And his room is off limits until the fire investigation team has completed their work. Stay out!" Officer Richards shook a warning finger at the group.

The officers walked off, leaving behind the frustrated students.

"I'm worried about Tyler. Why was his room on fire? It makes no sense." River sniffed.

"Yeah, none of us have any idea. He didn't have a roommate, and now his room is off limits, too." Desiree said.

Jodi chuckled as she chimed in. "Off limits maybe, but there are after hours..."

"Yeah, and how well did that work out for us when we wanted to check out my old room?"

"Diz, that was just 'cause Ms. Elmore found us."

Desiree grimaced. "She can be a nosy old lady."

"Guess that's part of her job."

Amelia theorized, "Probably something electrical. I've heard that fires have been started by putting a cell phone under your pillow and plugging it in to charge. I never do that."

Jonathan's phone rang, and he walked over to a corner to take the call, then rushed back to the group. "It's Tyler! I'll put him on speaker. Hey Tyler, you're on speaker now. Everyone is here."

A hoarse voice responded. "Thanks, Jon. Sorry about my voice. The doc said it's from smoke inhalation."

"No problem. We hear you just fine."

"When they gonna let you out of there?" River asked.

"Probably tomorrow. If my chest X-ray is clear. What're you guys doing?"

Jodi responded with a sigh, "Not much. Rehearsals have been cancelled, again. We're never getting out of here."

"Dang, sorry guys."

Amelia's soft voice piped up. "We wanted to come see you, but the police wouldn't let us."

Jonathan spoke next. "Speaking of which, they are on their way to talk to you about the fire. What can you tell us? They won't tell us anything."

"Not much. I was napping, trying to get rid of my headache. The smoke woke me and my trashcan was on fire. That is, the trash in my can was on fire. I tried to slide it further away, but it tipped over and then I tripped. That's all I remember till the firefighters dragged me out."

Desiree gasped. "Did you get burned badly?"

"Some on my legs. Guess they were closest to the fire. They're all bandaged up and the doc said it's second degree. Could be worse, just painful and probably some scarring."

River responded, "And you'll have a great story to tell all the girls."

"Aw, Riv. You know you're the only girl for me."

"You're embarrassing me." She giggled and blushed.

Tyler replied, "Yeah, like no one knew..." and everyone laughed.

"We'll let you go, and we all hope to see you tomorrow. Oh, and you can room with me or just get a new room."

"Thanks, Jon. Hope to see you all tomorrow."

Jonathan turned to the others. "He sounded pretty good, didn't he?"

Desiree shook her head. "Yeah, I'd be a basket case."

"Me, too," added Amelia.

Jodi turned to River. "So, you two have been carrying on in secret. Awesome!"

"I know. We didn't really try to keep it quiet, it just happened that way."

"Well, more power to you!"

Jonathan cleared his throat. "Am I the only one that thinks it's suspicious that his trash can just suddenly burst into flames? He doesn't smoke or play with matches."

Amelia paled. "Do you think this was intentional, like Cynthia's death?"

They all stared at the others in the group, wondering if one of them was a psycho. Then they all burst into laughter and Jon added, "Naw. There's no way." He looked around. "Is there?"

Chapter Ten

J odi's cell phone woke her early. "Yeah?" she growled.

"Sorry, didn't mean to wake you, but wanted to let you know that Jay is on his way there."

She bolted upright in bed. "No! Stevie, I asked you—"

"I didn't. He must have overheard something somewhere. Maybe Leathers, I'm sure he mentioned it to Romayne. You know they are an official couple now. I'm really sorry about this."

"No, it's not your fault. I knew what he'd do if he heard. When did he leave?"

"He called me after he left. Guess he knew I'd try to talk him out of it, so barring anything unforeseen, he should arrive in the next hour."

Jodi sighed. "Thanks for the warning, it's going to be a rough day."

"Yeah, I know. Again, sorry."

After clicking off, she jiggled Desiree. "Wake up."

"Huh?"

"You've gotta get up. We've got some damage control we need to do."

"Sleep. More sleep..."

She jiggled her again. "Not now, later. My brother is on his way here."

"My brother?"

"No, Diz! MY brother. You know, the cop!"

Desiree sat up and rubbed her eyes. "Why's he coming here?"

Jodi sat on the bed beside her. "Because he's a pain in my butt. Always has been, always will be." She pulled her arm. "C'mon, get up and get dressed. He could be here in less than an hour."

"Fine, just stop tugging on me."

Ten minutes later and they headed to the food truck area for their daily coffee and donut. They stopped when they realized the parking lot was empty. They spun round and still no trucks.

"What the—" Jodi sputtered.

"Where are they? I need my morning fix," Desiree pouted.

"I don't know. They were here yesterday."

Desiree looked at her watch. "Are we too early?"

"Nope. Seven every day, like clockwork. This makes no sense..." she paused. "Unless it's the police. I got the feeling they were going to interview the truck owners again. Maybe they ordered them to stay off campus until they're cleared?"

Desiree shrugged. "No idea, I just know I need my coffee and donut fix."

"Looks like we're going to have to settle for cafeteria coffee and a generic pastry."

"Blech!"

"Hey, it is what it is. I need to prepare myself for Jay's arrival. Let's go!"

The cafeteria was empty and the girls grabbed their coffees and Danish pastries from the vending machines.

Desiree took a sip of her coffee. "This is SO horrible."

"You've got to add cream and sugar. Makes it tolerable."

She poured three teaspoons of sugar and added cream before taking a sip. "Yeah, tolerable."

Desiree picked up the plastic wrapped Danish. "Now this, no way to make it tolerable."

"Yes there is. Hold on, I'll be right back." Jodi went to the self-serve counter, grabbed two plates, a couple of butters, and some silverware. Back at the table, she handed half of her haul to Dizzy. "Slather with butter, then microwave."

Two minutes later, they were enjoying hot buttered Danish pastries and sipping highly-doctored coffee.

"Not bad. Not bad at all. Where did you learn the buttered microwave tip? These things are like sweet cardboard otherwise."

Jodi laughed. "Big brother Jay."

☕

The two food truck vendors sat in the waiting area of the police station, waiting to be called back for their second interview. They were both sole owners of their trucks and were chatting about dealing with vendors and supply issues when Officer Standish popped around the corner.

"Mr. Edwards?"

The coffee truck vendor nodded.

"We're ready for you. Thank you for waiting."

He stood and told the other vendor, "Nice chatting with you again, Roberta. See you on campus."

"You, too, Mark. Hopefully, we can get back there tomorrow. This is cutting into profits."

He nodded and followed the officer into the interrogation room.

"Please have a seat. Can I get you something to drink? Coffee? Tea"

"Um, no offense, but I'll pass on the coffee."

Trent laughed. "No offense taken. Soda?"

"Diet cola would be fine."

Officer Mitchell Richards flipped through his notebook, waiting for Trent to return.

"Will this take long?" Mark asked.

"I don't believe so, just a few things we need to clarify. We appreciate your taking the time."

Mark shrugged. "Just being a good citizen. We were all shocked to hear about that girl's death."

Mitchell nodded.

"And then that strange fire..."

"How did you hear about that?"

"You haven't spent much time with twenty-something kids, have you? Everyone gossips. Of course, the fire trucks and ambulance were kind of a dead giveaway that something had happened. Is the boy okay?"

Trent returned and set the soda can in front of Mark, stopping further discussion.

He popped the tab and took a sip. 'Thanks. I'm used to having drinks on hand all day."

Mitchell started. "Are you friends with the other food truck vendors at the school?"

"More like acquaintances than friends. We chat, but some of us are in competition with the others. I'm the only coffee truck and fou-fou coffee is the thing nowadays, so no real competition for me. The vendors selling food, that's different. They need to keep things fresh and attract attention while retaining their existing customers."

"That makes sense. You were chatting with Ms. Crews while you waited?"

"Roberta? Yeah, she and I are the morning staples. I hang all day, but she usually pulls out just before lunch. Donuts are more of a morning thing, she says. I think she's wrong, but who am I to say?"

"Do you know if she is the only person who works her truck?"

"Actually, she had a guy helping her out last week. Said she needed to get some medical things resolved and hired a temp."

"Did you meet him?"

"He wasn't real friendly. Surprised me that he was doing this kind of work. You've gotta chat up folks, friend them. Smile, tell jokes, even flirt a little."

Trent hid his smile and Mitchell continued.

"So, did you even talk to him?"

"I tried. He just didn't seem to want to chat. Never shared much, so can't tell you much."

"Can you describe him?"

"Tall dude, about my height, but skinny. His hair looked bleached, too blond to be real. Maybe a buck-fifty."

"That all you remember? Any tattoos or scars you noticed?"

Mark scratched his neck as he thought. "He did have a tattoo on the back of his right hand. Looked like a music note. You know, like a cleft or whatever they call that squiggly thing."

"Clef note. Anything else?"

"Oh yeah, he had really weird eyes. Too light, wondered if he had them tattooed or something. I heard some folks do that."

Trent interjected, "When that is done, the entire eye is colored. There is no white area. Is that what you're saying?"

"No, just the pupils. They were such a light blue. Never seen anyone with eyes that color." He shrugged, "Contacts maybe?"

Trent continued. "I understand that Ms. Jodi Delgado bought coffee from you on a regular basis."

"You mean Gabby? Yeah, one of my best customers. She knows good coffee." He leaned forward. "Did you know she works in a coffee shop at home? I told her she could have a job with me anytime."

"What about Ms. Desiree Martinez? Did you ever meet her?"

"Are you kidding? Gabby and Dizzy are inseparable. I think they are sisters from another mother." He laughed at his joke.

"So they went to the food trucks together?"

"Every day, well, most days."

"Back to the donut truck. Do you remember the temp guy talking to them?"

"Nah, like I said. He kept to himself. But he did chat with the girl who died. Seems like they might have known each other."

"Can you think of anything else that might impact our investigation?"

Mark leaned back and crossed his legs. "Naw, but if I do, I know the drill. Contact you."

Mitchell replied, "Yes, please. Anything you remember about the three girls and the temp worker would be great."

The two officers stood. "Thank you for your time. You are free to return to the campus with your truck."

"Awesome. Thanks!"

As he walked out, Mitchell's phone rang. "Officer Richards." *pause* "Yes, sir. Just wrapped up one interview, one more to go." *pause* "What? You're not serious. We'll head right over there."

He turned to his partner. "There's been another incident at the school. Another contestant in this ridiculous contest has been injured."

Trent shook his head, "Murder, arson - now what?"

Chapter Eleven

❝ I'm so sorry you got called in. Really. It's nothing." Wesley tagged his ear as he glared at Ermine who just shrugged.

"That's alright. We'd rather come check things out, just to be safe. Let's finish our report and you can get on with your business." Officer Richards pulled out his notebook. "Now, who made the call to 9-1-1?"

Ermine stammered, "Me, um, I was, you know, I made the call." She turned red and glared at Wesley. "I know what I saw, and it was a hit and run." She shook her finger at him. "It's high time we cancelled this whole thing and sent everyone home."

Wesley cleared his throat. "We are NOT going—"

Officer Standish interrupted. "No one is going anywhere until this investigation is complete. Now please, calm down and answer Officer Richards' questions."

"Fine. I was looking out the hall window on the second floor—"

"Which building?" Trent interrupted again.

"This one. So, I was looking out the hall window and I saw a motor-cycle careening down the sidewalk."

"Do motorbikes on campus usually run on the sidewalk?" Trent asked.

"Oh my, heavens no! The sidewalk is for walking, just like it's name states." She primped her hair and smiled.

A clerk stuck her head in the door. "I'm sorry to interrupt, but there is a gentleman here demanding to see one of you."

Wesley responded, "Me or Ms. Elmore?"

"No, one of the officers."

"I'll take care of this. You continue," Mitchell nodded to Trent and followed the clerk.

"I wonder what—"

"Please focus, Ermine. We are wasting the officer's time." Wesley chided.

Ermine harrumphed, "Don't you scold me. I need to be accurate in what I tell Officer Standish." She turned back to Trent with a smile. "Now, where was I?"

"You were telling how you saw the motorcycle on the sidewalk."

Now it was Wesley who interrupted. "Now Ermine, was it really a motorcycle? Or maybe one of those little dirt bikes? Or even just one of the electric bicycles?" He turned to Trent. "It's important to make that distinction, right?"

Trent nodded.

"Well, it was kind of small, and since I was inside, I couldn't hear anything. But let me tell you, when he hit that boy..." She wiped a tear away. "It was so scary."

"And you know who the boy was?"

"No idea. By the time I got outside, they were both gone."

"Can you show me exactly where this happened?"

"Of course," she huffed. "Follow me."

As the trio exited the building, they noticed Officer Richards in the middle of an animated conversation with another man. Mitchell held up his hand to stop anyone from approaching so they continued on to the site of the hit and run.

"It was right here." Ermine pointed, then frowned. "Or was it over there?"

"Come on, Ermine. Focus! Where did it happen?"

She spun several times. "I'm so sorry. I thought it was here...or there, but now I'm not sure."

Trent sighed and put his notebook away. "I'm afraid there won't be further follow-up to this unless you come up with more information."

"But—"

"Don't argue with the officer. Just go back inside," Wesley urged.

"Fine. Whatever." She started towards the building but turned and shouted, "I still think we should shut down the school for the rest of the summer and send everyone home. For their own safety." She stormed off.

"I'm so sorry for the inconvenience, Officer Standish. She was the only person who thought they saw a hit and run. Who knows what she really saw. But it's obviously not a big deal. I do appreciate your prompt response to her call."

"That's my job, sir. Thank you for your assistance." Trent nodded and walked off towards his partner.

As he approached, the stranger shouted, "But she's my sister!"

"Everything okay here, Richards?"

Mitchell chuckled. "Jay, meet my partner, Trent Standish. Trent, this is Jay Delgado. He works for the Jumpers Hole police department. And..." he smiled at Jay, "he's Jodi Delgado's older brother."

Jay shook hands with Trent. "And I've come to take her home."

"And I already told him that wasn't possible. How'd you make out with the school officials?"

"She can't even pinpoint where the alleged hit and run occurred. Told them we'd place it on file but wouldn't pursue the investigation further."

"Sounds good to me." Mitchell turned back to Jay. "As I was saying, until we close the investigation into the death of Ms. Peabody, no one is going anywhere."

Jay shook his head. "These are just kids!"

"No, they're not. They're all eighteen or older. Adults in the legal sense."

"Look, I understand. But with multiple incidents, wouldn't they be safer at home? You have all their contact information. I mean—"

"I'm sorry. This is our jurisdiction and our investigation. You're welcome to talk to your sister and even stay in town, but please do not interfere in any way."

"Can you at least tell me how the victim died?"

Trent nudged his partner. "You might as well tell him. I suspect it will get leaked before much longer. The mayor is really pressuring the chief for more information to release to the public. Can't keep it quiet forever."

"Fine. The deceased was killed due to eating the donuts that 'no one', evidently, gave to her. The ingredients contained both sesame seeds and sesame oil. Our victim was deadly allergic to both."

"I've never heard of that before. Nuts, yes. But sesame?"

"I know. It was finely ground, so we suspect she never noticed it until it was too late."

"Was the school aware of this allergy?"

"Yes, and according to them, everyone on staff knew. In addition, all the students were made aware of the allergy."

"I take it she didn't have an epinephrine auto-injector? I know my dad is allergic to bees and always carries his."

"After talking to her parents, it appears she was rather lax about it. She should have always carried one, but we didn't find it in her room or with her belongings."

"Still rebellious, I guess." Trent broke in.

Jay chuckled. "Yeah, they may not be kids per se, but they can still act like them. Okay, so nothing out of the ordinary. Just donuts aimed at killing her."

Mitchell continued, "Initially we thought she was poisoned, but when the toxicology report came back clear, we authorized an autopsy. The medical examiner is a school chum of our chief and he got right to it."

Trent added, "Good thing. We were heading out to track down the roommate, Desiree—"

"My sister's friend?"

"Yes, we thought she might have been the actual target. Now we know better and can refocus our investigation."

Mitchell spoke again. "But that's not the only strange thing. There was a fire in the room of one of the finalists. The fire investigator is looking into arson."

"Wow! Was anyone injured?" Jay asked.

"One student, minor burns and smoke inhalation. Nothing too serious. He'll fully recover."

"That's good." Jay saw someone headed in their direction. "Um, that looks like my sister headed here with a storm cloud over her head. Thanks, guys. I'll give you a shout if I find out anything." Seeing the scowl on Mitchell's face, he added, "But I won't be purposely doing any investigation."

"Jay Delgado! What are you doing here? You should be—"

He wrapped Jodi in a hug. "Hi Gabby. I love you, too."

The two officers chuckled as they walked back to their car.

Chapter Twelve

❝ Wesley, I mean it. We need to shut down for the rest of the summer. Send all the students home and lay off the staff." Ermine leaned towards her boss and glared.

Wesley seemed to be unfazed. "Sit down, Ermine. Don't get your panties all in a wad."

She frowned but sat, tapping her fingers on the arm of the wooden chair. "I'm serious! I mean, think about it. We've got one dead student, another injured, and who knows what happened to the third one."

He cocked his head. "Third one?"

"You know, the hit and run."

He scowled. "The police didn't seem overly concerned."

"Well, I am." She slammed her hand on his desk. "You need to take action before someone else dies."

"We can't, it'll ruin our reputation. Just give the police time. They'll figure it out. The Peabody girl died from an allergic reaction. There's no reason to think that it's murder. And the Hawkins boy, well, he probably tossed a cigarette butt in his trash."

She snorted. "More likely to be a marijuana butt."

"Whatever. The point is, we have no valid reason to shut things down. In fact, I'd like to move up the timetable, declare the grand winner, and—"

"Just send everyone home!"

He sighed. "You do realize that's up to the police."

"Then they better get off their butts and close these investigations. Nothing nefarious has happened." She got up to leave, but continued, "But I still think it's dangerous for everyone to stay. They should all leave. Now!"

"But you just said nothing nefarious—"

"Oh, just shut up." She stormed out of the office and slammed the door behind her.

"I don't know why I put up with her." He shook his head, picked up the phone and dialed. "Chief Davison, please." *pause* "Hey Dennis, it's Wesley Sherman over at the school." *pause* "Yeah, I'm fine thanks. How's the family?" *pause* "That's great. I'm calling about Officers Richards and Standish. They're conducting an investigation here, and I wondered if you could light a fire under them. I'd really like to get things resolved and closed so we can finalize our scholarship competition. Then everyone can go home." *pause* "Thanks, I knew I could count on you. I'll see you at the club this weekend. I still owe you a whipping on the golf course." He hung up, made a note on his calendar, and leaned back in his chair for a nap.

☕

"This is what I got from what the officers told me. One. The Peabody girl died from an anaphylactic reaction to sesame." Jodi started to interrupt, but Jay held up his hand. "Wait till I'm done. There was ground up sesame seeds as well as sesame oil in the donut she ate as well as the uneaten donuts. They are still working on figuring out who put the donuts in her room. Until they discovered the sesame and allergies, they were considering the possibility that you, Desiree, might have been the intended target. Two. There's the Tyler Hawkins incident. The fire in his room is still under investigation and considered suspicious. And three happened today. A hit and run was reported, but they found no evidence of anything actually happening. That about wraps it up." He sat back and waited for his sister to argue with him.

But she agreed. "That's pretty much the same as we know, except we hadn't heard about Cyndi's actual cause of death." She leaned across the table. "We need to find out where those donuts came from. Have they interviewed Roberta?'

"Roberta?"

"The donut lady. She owns Rolling Dough."

Desiree added, "And don't forget that sketchy guy that filled in."

"All they said was they had interviewed the food truck vendors. Nothing specific." Jay scratched the back of his neck. "Interesting. Sketchy guy? What else can you tell me about him? When did he work? What did he look like? Do you know his name?"

Jodi held up her hand and laughed. "Whoa there, Columbo. One question at a time."

"Fine. Tell me about this sketchy guy."

"Diz, you always bought the donuts, so you need to answer."

Desiree leaned back and closed her eyes. "Initially, it was just the owner, Roberta, who worked the truck. But she hurt her back and called in someone to work."

"Sketchy guy?" Jay quipped.

"Yeah, sketchy guy. He had shifty eyes and was tall and really thin. Like maybe over six-feet and..." She paused. "And maybe one hundred and fifty pounds."

"Age?"

She shrugged. "Maybe our age? I know he rode a bicycle."

"I thought he drove the donut food truck?"

"He did, but there was an old bicycle strapped to the back of it. Roberta never had one when she drove, so I kinda figured it was his." Jay made a note as she continued. "He had sandy colored hair, not long, but not short. Kept falling over his eyes. Oh, and he always wore a dirty old baseball cap."

"Logo? Insignia?"

"No, just dirty blue, almost grey."

"Did he tell you his name?"

"Not initially, but I think finally he did. I tend to be a blabbermouth with strangers, so I kept pestering him."

"Name?"

She frowned. "I can't remember right now."

"How many days did he work?"

She tapped her chin. "Let me see. Probably less than a week before we found Cyndi."

"And since?"

"I think he's still working. Roberta told Mark she'd be out for maybe a month. She really wrenched her back."

Jay sighed. "Mark?"

Jodi giggled. "Mark owns the Cool Beans coffee truck. He's a really neat guy." She paused. "For someone older." She winked at Desiree.

Jay sighed again. "Did you ever see him talking with Ms. Peabody?" He quickly added, "The nameless sketchy guy, not Mark the coffee guy."

"Cyndi? No—"

Jodi interrupted. "I did. You had already gotten the donuts. I was late getting the coffees, and I told you to go ahead. As I left, I saw Cyndi walking up to the donut truck. When I looked back, she was chatting with sketchy guy. I thought it looked like they knew each other."

Jay scribbled another note. "Sounds like I need to talk to this nameless sketchy guy."

"Um, aren't you supposed to let Officers Richards and Standish do the investigation?"

Jay laughed. "Sure, and they'd do the same if they were in a similar situation in my neck of the woods. I just want to chat. Nothing official. He might open up more that way."

Chapter Thirteen

"Boy, the Chief sure chewed us a new one." Trent Standish handed a go-cup of coffee from the cardboard carrier to his partner, Mitchell.

"I'm not surprised. The Peabody girl's parents are pressing him to arrest someone for the murder of their daughter."

"Yeah, I suppose. I'm not a parent, but..." he shook his head. "I really can't imagine what they are going through."

"Good thing Ms. Crews was understanding about the incident and waited for us to return for her interview."

"And maybe we will find out about the guy who was working for her on the donut truck."

They walked back into the waiting area of the police station. "Ms. Crews, again we thank you for your patience. Officer Standish brought coffee. Would you like one?"

Trent pointed out the creamers and sugar on the sideboard. "We have the fixings here."

Roberta nodded and took a cup from the carrier. "Thank you so much. I can really use this right now. I'm not getting much sleep with this back pain."

"Again, thank you. We're going to talk in here." Mitchell pointed to the adjoining conference room.

Roberta stirred three sugar packets into her coffee and took a sip. "Not bad. Did you get it from the coffee truck?"

Trent laughed. "I wish, but since we had just finished our interview with Mr. Edwards, he wasn't on the campus."

She sat and sipped again. "Campus? You were called back to the school then?"

"Yes, but it turned out to be nothing."

"Well, that's good. So, what do you need to know?"

Mitchell flipped open his notebook and scanned a few pages before starting. "I understand you've had a temp worker while you recovered from your back injury. Is that correct?"

"It is. A young man referred by another student."

"Do you remember who referred him?"

"Not really. After a while, they all blur together. Only a few ever stood out. Like the regulars who took time to chat with me."

"Ms. Martinez was a regular, right?"

She laughed. "Every day since the competition began. Not that she was ever on time. She often caught me just as I was getting ready to close." She paused. "No, wait. Those were the days she visited twice. Sorry, old age and a poor memory." She took another sip of her coffee. "Once the finals began, she was a morning regular. Like clockwork. Always got a dozen mixed."

"And the victim, Ms. Peabody?"

"No, I can't say as I could have picked her out of a crowd. So I don't know if she ever visited the truck."

"Do you make your own donuts, or do you get them from a bakery?"

She sniffed. "I make my own. No way are production donuts ever going to be as good as mine."

Trent interrupted "Do you ever use sesame oil or seeds in your donut production?"

"Heavens, no. Why would I ever do that? If I were still selling bagels on the truck, then yes for the sesame seed bagels. But donuts?" She shivered. "Never. I can't see anyone doing that."

Mitchell and Trent exchanged looks and Mitchell asked, "What about after you hurt your back? Who supplies your donuts?"

"Well, the man I hired for the truck. He makes them. He had experience from working in a bakery."

"Do you have a commercial facility for making the donuts?"

"The truck IS the facility. I didn't want the overhead of leasing or owning a building, so I had the truck outfitted with everything we need."

"Doesn't it take hours to make donuts?"

"Only the yeast ones. The cake donuts take maybe thirty minutes."

"So you only sell cake donuts?"

"For a bit, after I was first out. Now I make the dough early in the morning, let it rest for an hour. My guy picks it up around seven, does the final proofing and then fries them. That's how we have so many varieties. Of course, they're not all available all days. One day will be glazed and chocolate covered. Another will be filled. Then a day with plain and crullers, with or without sugar and cinnamon. Then a day for different icings. Variety keeps them coming back."

"I see."

"When I was at 100%, I made it all in the truck. Getting up at five in the morning was never an issue. I don't need a lot of sleep. Well, I didn't. You know that saying, getting old ain't for sissies."

"To restate, your worker comes to your home every morning to pick up the dough and finishes the process in the food truck."

"You got it."

"Before that, he made cake donuts only. In the truck. By himself."

She nodded. "For about a week after I hired him. Then I got back into the swing of things." She leaned forward. "Do you suspect him of having something to do with that girl's death?"

"We're just getting all our facts straight."

While Mitchell made another note, Trent asked, "Do you have the contact information for this temp worker?"

"It's on my phone. Hold on." She burrowed through her purse, pulling out her cell phone. Scrolling through her contact list, she stopped and handed it to Trent. "Here it is. Ethan Nethers."

"Thank—"

"But he isn't working for me anymore. You know that, right?"

Mitchell stopped writing. "No, we didn't know that. What happened?"

"I'm really not sure. He called me up a couple days ago and said he had found another temp worker with experience. He agreed to take over my duties."

"Oh?"

"But the other temp never called or showed, so I figured I felt well enough to go back to work. The truck was closed today, but I'll be there tomorrow."

The officers exchanged glances and stood. Mitchell extended his hand. "Thank you for coming and waiting for us. We appreciate all your assistance."

"Oh, it's no matter. Now you boys stop by anytime, and I'll give you a free sample donut. Just one. Wouldn't want you to get in any trouble."

They chuckled as Trent escorted her out the door. "We will certainly stop by, but we will pay for our donuts. The offer is appreciated though."

Once she was gone, he turned back to Mitchell. "Don't you think it's suspicious that he replaced himself with another temp worker?"

Mitchell shrugged. "Maybe yes, maybe no. Could just have gotten a real job. We'll find out when we interview him."

Chapter Fourteen

Jay pulled into the trailer park just as the two officers were exiting their vehicle.

"What are you doing here?" Mitchell demanded.

Jay smirked. "Probably the same thing as you."

"You planned on talking to Ethan Nethers?"

"Huh, so that's his name. All I had was the address."

"And..."

Jay chuckled. "Yup. I wanted to talk to him. I know I have no jurisdiction, but my sister is involved. You understand."

It was Trent's turn to chuckle as he nudged his partner. "You know what sisters are like, right?"

Mitchell sighed. "Fine. You can sit in on the interview. That's all. No questions. Agreed?"

Jay nodded. "Agreed." He surveyed the park, noting the deterioration of most of the trailers. "Not the upscale part of town, is it?"

Trent grimaced. "Unfortunately, it's a necessity. Once the cheap motels are full, the owner here rents the trailers by the week to the service workers that come to work. He doesn't do much to keep it updated, as you can see."

Mitchell added, "But it's the only other place the workers can afford. You come from a tourist area, too, don't you? How does your town handle the influx of workers during the season?"

"The town built a dorm-type building and we rent it at a reasonable cost. First dibs always go to the service workers. The tourists in our neck of the woods come from neighboring towns, too, so the motel needs are lighter. But hey, let's go get this guy and talk to him."

"Right." Mitchell checked his notebook. "It's that one over there. Number 1475." He pointed to an aging Airstream at the far end of the park. An equally aging pickup was parked beside it.

Trent knocked on the door and stepped back as Mitchell called out, "Ethan Nethers. It's the police. We'd like to talk to you."

The door squeaked as it opened and a scruffy haired head peered out. "Yeah? Why?"

"It's about your work for Roberta Crews."

Ethan squinched up his face. "Roberta who?"

"Crews. You worked on her food truck, Rolling Dough."

"Oh yeah. I don't work there anymore. I quit."

"We'd like you to come down to the station and chat with us for a bit. Nothing official, we just have a few questions."

"Right now?"

"That would be best."

"Ah, okay, I guess. Let me put on some shoes and turn off my oven."

"Sure." Mitchell turned to the others as the door closed. "That seemed almost too easy."

Before anyone could respond, the door opened again. "This have anything to do with Cyndi Peabody?"

"Yes, it does."

"Then I'm not coming. I've got nothing to say." Ethan slammed the door.

"Now what?" Trent asked his partner.

"Let me try." Getting a nod from Mitchell, Jay knocked on the door. "Ethan, I'm Jay Delgado and I don't work for the police here. But I'm the brother of Jodi Delgado and her best friend is Desiree Martinez. You might not know it, but Ms. Martinez was Cynthia Peabody's roommate and the one who found her. We're all here to trying to find out more about Ms. Peabody's death. Someone reported that you knew her. We just want to talk."

The door opened a couple of inches. "Just talk?"

"Yes. Just talk. And we can do it here or at the station. You're not being accused of anything. We just thought you might be more comfortable with us at the station rather than us invading your privacy here."

Mitchell mouthed "That's good..." to Trent.

"Oh, um. Okay. Like, I'm not charged with anything. You're not arresting me."

"No, nothing like that. We just need to talk to anyone who knew the victim. You'd like to find out who did this to her, wouldn't you?"

"Yeah. Okay. I'll be out in a minute." The door closed again.

Mitchell smiled. "That was impressive."

Jay shrugged. "Delgado charm."

The door opened, and Ethan stepped out. "Can I ride with him?" He pointed to Jay.

The three men nodded.

☕

"Jay just texted me. They found our nameless sketchy guy and are taking him to the police station right now." Jodi set her phone down and smiled at Desiree. "He said the guy's name is Ethan Nethers."

"Huh, wonder what they will find out."

"Don't know, but Jay said he initially refused to talk to them as soon as they mentioned Cyndi's name."

"That's suspicious."

"I agree. Maybe they'll get this resolved today and we can get on with the competition."

"Sure would be nice."

"What would be nice?" River walked up to their table along with Jonathan.

Desiree grinned. "The police are interviewing that creepy, sketchy guy who was working on the Rolling Dough truck."

River scratched his head. "Okay, but what would be nice?"

"That maybe we can finally finish this competition and head home. I don't know about you, but I'm so over all this. I just want to be done."

River sat. "Yeah, my folks are bugging me to just leave, but I'm not ready."

"Me neither," chimed both Jodi & Desiree.

"Well, I just want everyone to know who the best is, and it's me!" Jonathan put a foot up on a chair and beat his chest.

"Sit down, you jerk," River admonished.

"Nah, I'm gonna grab a sandwich and go watch a movie. Anyone want to join me?"

"What movie?" everyone asked, then laughed.

"It's a toss-up between *Fame* and *School of Rock*."

The response was unanimous: "*School of Rock*!"

"What's all this ruckus? I thought you students were better behaved than that," Ermine Elmore scolded.

"Sorry, Ms. Elmore. We were just celebrating. We're about to leave." Desiree stood along with the others.

"Why are you celebrating? There hasn't been much to cheer about for a while now."

"My brother texted me to let me know they found the sketchy guy from the donut truck, and the police are getting ready to interrogate him."

"Oh my, that is good news. Well, then. Go on with you. Just keep it to inside voices, please."

Chapter Fifteen

❝ Can I get you something to drink?" Trent asked Ethan as they entered the interrogation room. "Coffee, water, soda?"

Ethan grinned. "Dr. Pepper?"

"Hey, you think this is some swanky specialty restaurant?" Trent frowned, then laughed. "Just kidding. Yeah, we got it. Be right back." He nodded to Mitchell and got a thumbs up back. "Coffee it is."

Mitchell pointed to a chair as he sat. "This is just a casual conversation, Ethan. We're just interviewing everyone who had interactions with the students in the competition at the school."

Ethan nodded as he took the canned soda from Trent, who added, "All conversations are automatically recorded to protect you. Understand?"

Ethan nodded again, took a long swig of the soda and set the can down. "I got nothing to hide. Go ahead and grill me." He crossed his arms.

"I'm curious why you initially refused to talk to us?" Mitchell asked.

"Well, 'cause, um," he blushed. "Cyndi was my ex-girlfriend, and I thought you suspected me."

Outside the room, Jay gasped as he watched through the one-way window.

"I see. So you did know the victim, Cynthia Peabody."

"Yeah, we dated through high school."

"When did you break up?"

"She went off to college and sent me a text saying we were over." He slumped in the chair.

"I bet that made you angry."

"Sure, wouldn't you be angry? I mean, not even a phone call." He leaned forward. "We dated for four years. We had plans." More softly, he added, "I had plans."

Trent picked up the questioning. "What kind of plans?"

Ethan shrugged. "You know, plans. Like kids, and marriage, and a house. Plans."

"So she dumped you. How long ago?"

"A couple months ago, I guess."

"Did she say why?"

"Not really. I figured she met someone. I don't know. She just said she didn't want to see me anymore."

"So that's why you took the job on the Rolling Dough truck?"

"Yeah. I knew she was in the competition. I just wanted to make sure she was okay."

"The owner, Roberta Crews, said she thought another student recommended you. She couldn't remember who it was. Do you have any idea who might have done that?"

Ethan shook his head.

Mitchell slapped his hand on the table, making Ethan jump. "So you decided if you couldn't have her, then no one else could either."

"No! I wouldn't hurt her. I loved her."

Trent nudged Mitchell, "How many times have we heard that story..."

"No, I mean it. The last time I talked to her, we agreed we could still be friends. I quit the donut truck when I heard she was dead. You need to find out who killed her. It wasn't me!"

Trent smiled smugly. "How do you know she was killed? Maybe she died of natural causes."

"People talk. All the time." Ethan leaned closer to the officers. "But no one told me how she died. Was she shot? Stabbed? Poisoned?" He leaned back. "Jeesh, guys. Maybe I could help if I knew more."

Mitchell exchanged glances with Trent before responding. "Interesting. So you'd like to help us." Ethan nodded. "Were you aware if Ms. Peabody had any health issues?"

"Not really. She was pretty athletic for a musician." He sighed. "She loved to run."

"What about allergies?"

"You mean like bee stings?

"Sure. Or food allergies."

"Not that I knew about or that she talked about."

Trent interjected, "Was she a fan of South Asian, Middle Eastern, Mediterranean, or Caribbean cuisine?"

Ethan snorted. "You gotta be kidding me. We were high school kids. Burgers and fries kind of dates."

"Ethan, can you think of anyone who might have wanted to hurt Ms. Peabody?"

"No, she, um, she..." Ethan sniffed, "she was nice to everyone." He paused. "Well, most of the time."

"Oh? What makes you say that?"

"We talked when she came to the donut truck. I got the idea she really wanted to win the competition."

"That's all you talked about?"

He nodded. "Yeah, she wasn't sorry for our break-up, but she told me..." His voice cracked as he continued, "She told me she was sorry about how she did it. I told her I forgave her. So like I said, we were friends."

Mitchell unexpectedly stood and shook Ethan's hand. "We appreciate your cooperation. We'll contact you if we need any additional information. You can go now."

Jay entered after Ethan left the room.

Mitchell asked, "So what do you think?"

"I think he's a lovesick kid and had nothing to do with it. What are—"

"Hold on, I've got a message to call Roberta Crews. She remembered something." Mitchell punched the number into his phone. "Ms. Crews, this is Officer Mitchell Richards returning your call. You said you remembered something. Would you please give me a call back as soon as possible? Thank you." Turning to the others he said, "Voicemail. No idea what she remembered, but we should talk to her as soon as we can."

"So, where do we go from here?" Jay asked.

Mitchell sighed. "Unless something new turns up, and soon, I think we've hit a dead end."

Trent added, "Well then, let's hope the information from Ms. Crews gives us some direction."

☕

Roberta heard her phone ring, but she was elbow deep in dough and let it go to voicemail. Once she had washed her hands and dried them on her apron, she dug the phone out of her apron's pocket. "Dang it, missed him," she mumbled while hitting the voicemail icon. "Guess I should just go down there." She looked around her kitchen and shrugged. "Later. I doubt it's important anyway." She returned to her new passion, kolache rolls.

Two hours later, she was done. She surveyed the trays of filled rolls, ready to sell. She had discovered the recipe while browsing for ideas to expand her offerings. Yeast rolls filled with fruit, cheese, and sometimes nuts. They originated in the Czech Republic and were served at church dinners, bazaars and family gatherings. As the Czech community immigrated to the states, they brought the pastry with them. They were soon Americanized, and recipes with variations were available all over the internet. She had decided to start with the basic apricot-filled kolache. If these sold well on her truck, she planned to expand into fig, peach, blueberry, strawberry, and maybe even prune fillings. These might end up being made for a second truck run, hitting the early dinner crowd at various spots around town.

Looking at her watch, she decided it was too late to head to the police station, so she dug out her phone to make another call to Officer Richards. Two rings and he picked up. "Officer Richards? It's Roberta Crews."

"Yes, sorry for the phone tag. You said you remembered something?"

"Yes. You had asked me who recommended Ethan Nethers as a temp worker. I thought it was one of the students, but then I remembered it was the school counselor, Ermine Elmore."

"Interesting. Did she say how she knew Mr. Nethers?"

"I'm not positive, but she said something about a friend or relative that might have mentioned him. I'm sorry, I'm just not sure. You should ask her."

"We will and thank you. Sorry for the phone tag."

Roberta chuckled. "I was elbow deep in dough when you called. I'm trying something new."

"Oh?"

"Kolaches. I'm hoping they will be good for a later in the day snack. So many people associate donuts with mornings. I need to branch out more."

"I'm not sure what that is, but I promise to try one if you run the truck by the station. Tell Cecily I want two of them. She'll pay for them and stash them for me and Trent."

"I'll do that. And if you like them, spread the word."

"You know it. Thank you, Ms. Crews." He disconnected and turned to Trent and Jay. "Sounds like we need to talk to Ms. Elmore at the school."

Chapter Sixteen

" So, where does that leave us?" Jay asked the two officers.

Trent shrugged. Mitchell pulled out his notebook and made some notes as he answered. "The only thing we can do now is interview everyone at the school again."

"Do you really think that will provide anything new?" Trent asked.

"I don't know, but we're running out of suspects. The ex-boyfriend was at the top of my list, but I've pretty much crossed him off now."

"Why? He was upset she dumped him," Jay interjected.

"I just don't see him as the killer. Someone wanted Ms. Peabody out of the picture. He wanted a future with her. I think we need to start at the top and work our way down the list, talking to everyone involved in the competition. Again."

"Let's grab some lunch," Trent suggested as he and Mitchell headed out the door. "You coming?" he asked Jay.

"Sure, thanks. Wasn't sure I was invited."

"All hands on deck, as my Pa would have said."

"Navy guy?"

Trent chuckled. "How'd you guess?"

"I'll take my car and meet you...where?"

"Sophie's Diner, it's in the middle of downtown."

"I'll follow you."

"Great, Mitchell's driving, so I'll call the school on the way over and set things up for another round of talks."

The diner was almost full when they arrived, but they found a corner booth with enough room for the three of them. In between bites of their lunch, they reviewed what they knew so far, including the fire in Tyler Hawkins's room.

Jay shook his head. "There just doesn't seem to be any connection between the three incidents."

"I agree," Mitchell responded. "We have one death involving foul play, one accidental fire, and one non-existent hit and run. Nothing ties them together."

"Maybe we're trying too hard. It could all be coincidental."

Trent frowned. "I don't believe in coincidence."

"Did you get the school meet arranged?"

Trent looked at his watch. "We've got twenty minutes before everyone we previously interviewed is gathered up. We need to wrap this up."

"Go ahead and pay. We'll meet you out front. I want to ask Jay a question."

Trent nodded, picked up the check, and headed to the cashier.

"Have you heard anything more from your sister? Anything the contestants might have mentioned that could mean something?"

"Afraid not. I think they're all just ready to finish the competition and head home."

"Yeah, that's what I thought. Figured I should check, just in case."

☕

"I don't understand why they have to come and bother us again." Ermine paced in Wesley's office. "We need to get this all over and done with. They don't know who's behind it all." She slammed her hand on Wesley's desk. "That means all the students are in danger. You need to shut this down and send everyone home." She straightened and crossed her arms. "Just end it. That's your job. Keep everyone safe."

Wesley had flinched when Ermine had banged his desk, but he wasn't swayed. "We have to see this through. These students have put a lot into the competition and to send everyone home without declaring a winner and awarding the grand prize...well, that would just be criminal."

"There is a criminal, but we have no idea who it is. I walk around here on eggshells, afraid of what might happen next. Another fire? A bomb? Another dead body?" She shivered. "I'm pleading with you. Cancel everything and send everyone home. Promise them they can come back next summer and be in the semi-finals automatically."

He sighed and shook his head. "You do make some sense, but I just can't do it. Let's see what the police come up with this go round. Maybe they'll have some good news for us."

Ermine spun around and muttered as she exited, "That's not very likely..."

Wesley hollered after her, "Tell them I'll be there in ten minutes."

She waved in acknowledgment.

Chapter Seventeen

The students piled into the cafeteria, voices chattering about why they had been called together. As soon as one person spoke their thoughts, another would chime in with contradictions. The finalists in the competition sat grouped together as the others scattered around the room.

"Gabby, do you think they're going to tell us who killed Cyndi?" Desiree asked. "Has your brother told you anything?"

"Your guess is as good as mine, but it sure would be nice if that happened. Nothing from Jay."

"I heard it was the ex-boyfriend. He was broken-hearted and killed her in a fit of jealousy." River made gesture mimicking a neck being sliced.

"Don't be so dramatic. You're such a drama queen sometimes," Tyler chided as Amanda giggled. He turned and frowned at her. "And you're no help, you just egg her on."

Jodi shushed the others. "Guys, hush up. Mr. Sherman and Ms. Elmore are coming in."

Wesley stood in the center of the room to address the group. "Thank you all for coming. I know this process is getting tedious, but we need to continue to assist the police in every way we can during their investigation. They should be here shortly and will be conducting interviews one more time."

Under her breath Ermine muttered, "They should just close the books on this, and we should tell everyone to go home. This is so ridiculous."

Wesley scowled as he continued addressing the room. "If you have any questions or concerns, please bring them to me." He looked at Ermine again. "Only me. Thank you."

"Send them home, Wesley." Ermine tugged on Wesley's arm. "They're tired. I'm tired. Just send them home!"

"Ermine, shush! Why don't you go back to your office? I'll let the officers know where you are when they are ready to talk to you."

"We don't need them to tell us this was all accidental. We know that. Right? Please send everyone—"

The room was silent as everyone listened to the conversation.

"That's enough! Leave now, before you upset the students further."

Ermine stormed out of the room leaving a confused group behind.

"Please, everyone. Everything is fine. As Ms. Elmore said, we're all tired of this. But, we do hope to have some resolution soon." He walked over to the table where the finalists sat. "I want to extend my apologies to you all specifically. I'm afraid Ms. Elmore is a bit overwhelmed by everything that has gone on here. I truly hope the police can put this matter to rest today, and we can finalize the competition so we can announce the results in another couple of days. Thank you all for your patience."

The group nodded in unison as Jodi responded. "Thank you, Mr. Sherman. I'm sure everything will be resolved soon. Don't worry about us," she smiled at her tablemates, "we're all doing just fine. We appreciate everything the school has done to accommodate us."

Wesley nodded and moved to the next table.

Desiree leaned in close to the table and whispered, "Do you think Ms. Elmore is having a nervous breakdown?"

River replied, "I heard her talking to herself this morning."

"What was she saying?" Jodi asked.

"Pretty much what we just heard her telling Mr. Sherman. That he needs to shut the school down and send everyone home."

"Why would she say that?" Tyler asked.

"Who knows? She's always seemed a bit off to me," River answered.

Desiree cocked her head. "Off? In what way?"

River shrugged. "Just different. At least different from when we first got here. Then she was like my Aunt Jo. Nag, nag, nag."

The group laughed, but stopped as the three officers walked into the cafeteria. Jay caught his sister's eye and nodded as they approached the middle of the room where Mitchell spoke first. "Thank you all for coming in today. We will be calling you in, one by one, for another interview." A groan rose from the room. "I understand your frustration. I know you are all tired and want answers. We would love to have some, but as of right now, we have nothing new to share."

Trent spoke next. "When I call your name, please follow us for your interview. Desiree Martinez."

Two hours later, the officers dismissed the students. As they stood in the empty cafeteria, they went over their results.

"Well, that didn't seem to provide any new answers," Jay said.

Trent shook his head as Mitchell responded. "No, but I'm not really surprised. Ready to tackle Mr. Sherman and Ms. Elmore?"

"Sure," Trent and Jay replied.

☕

The officers found Ermine huddled over her desk, tossing paperwork onto the floor and muttering to herself.

Trent spoke first. "Ms. Elmore? Are you okay?"

"What does it look like? Does it look like I'm okay? He won't listen to me. I've begged and I've pleaded. But no, he thinks he knows better. Well, he doesn't. I do." She opened a ledger book, tore out some pages, and tossed them into the wastebasket. Some missed and fell to the floor. "He just doesn't know. He doesn't understand."

The three officers exchanged puzzled looks. Concerned, Mitchell asked, "Understand what, Ms. Elmore?"

"It's over. We're done. Close the door. Maybe next year. But he won't do it. I've tried and tried to make him understand." She tore out several more ledger pages and tossed them down.

Trent knelt beside her and reached out to touch her arm. She yanked it away. "You boys, shoo! Just go! Away with you. I'm too busy to talk. Go home."

Trent stood and waited for Mitchell to react.

"I'm sorry, Ms. Elmore, but we can't do that. We need to talk to you one more—"

"I'm too busy. Can't you see that?" Her voice raised an octave and cracked as she continued with a small sob. "I'm too busy. I've got to take care of this. All of this." She continued to tear out more pages from the ledger, ripped them half, and tossed them towards the overflowing wastebasket. "Got to finish this before the police find out." She pulled out several desk drawers, muttering, "Where are those matches? Can't find anything when I need it."

Mitchell whispered to Trent, "Go get Mr. Sherman. Now!"

Trent nodded and hurried off, returning with Wesley.

"Ermine, what's going on here?" he demanded. "You're making a mess. Stop it right now!"

She looked up at Wesley with tear-filled eyes. "I told you to send everyone home, but you wouldn't listen. It's all your fault."

"What's my fault?"

"I had to do it. I had to protect the school's reputation."

"Do what, Ermine?"

"I didn't mean to. It was an accident." She started sobbing. As her words sunk in, Wesley blanched.

Mitchell cleared his throat. "Ms. Elmore, I'm afraid you need to come with us to the station. We can have a chat there. Mr. Sherman can take care of things here."

She nodded and wiped her wet cheeks. As they led her away, she continued mumbling, "It was an accident. I didn't mean it. Just a warning. That was all. But he wouldn't listen. Why wouldn't he listen?"

Chapter Eighteen

The six final contestants sat around the table waiting for the official update from Mr. Sherman.

River frowned. "I can't believe Ms. Elmore was the killer."

"Is that actually what Jay told you?" Desiree asked Jodi.

"Yup! I can't believe it either."

"But why?" Tyler asked. "And what about the fire in my room?"

"He said she confessed to that, too. But she swore she didn't intend for you to get hurt. It just got out of hand."

"Big time!" He sighed and shook his head.

"Yeah, so why?" Amanda prompted.

"Well, seems she had been borrowing money from the school—"

"Embezzling?" the group chimed.

Jodi nodded. "Turns out she was addicted to gambling on-line and needed the money to keep betting. She kept thinking she would win and pay it back before anyone knew. But then it was too late. The school needed to pay out the scholarship funds, and the money wasn't there."

"And Cyndi?" Desiree asked.

"She swore she didn't mean to kill her, just make her sick. I guess she underestimated how severe Cyndi's allergy was and it killed her."

"That's really scary. What's going to happen to her?" River asked.

"Jay said they were charging her with second-degree murder of Cyndi, aggravated assault for harming Tyler in the fire, and making a false report of a crime for the hit and run incident."

"Wow! That's pretty serious," Desiree responded.

Jodi nodded again. "Yeah, but Jay said all the charges will probably be pled down to manslaughter and simple assault. At least, that's what he suspects. Regardless, she'll go to jail for a long time."

Desiree crossed her arms and slumped in the chair. "Humph, she deserves it."

"I wonder what will happen to us. I mean, we all won our divisions. There's that money. I wonder if we'll even get that..." River sighed.

"Who knows? I guess we'll learn more when Mr. Sherman addresses us this afternoon."

The group nodded in agreement.

☕

"Thank you all for your patience and cooperation with the police department. As you may have already heard, Ms. Elmore was arrested and charged with the death of Ms. Cynthia Peabody and several other charges as well. Unfortunately, the circumstances of why this happened have affected the competition and pending scholarships. As originally stated, each of you finalists were to receive a five thousand dollar cash award and the grand prize winner would have received twenty-five thousand dollars." He looked around the room before continuing. "I am sorry to say, we are unable to present any cash awards."

The group gasped, and he held up his hand. "But, in lieu of the cash awards, the board has authorized me to present each of the six finalists with a ten thousand dollar scholarship to our school, the Whisper Peak Institute of Music. There is no expiration date on these scholarships, so you may feel free to continue your current college educations. You may return here at any time that works for you."

As the group broke into applause, Jodi raised her hand.

"Ms. Delgado, you have a question?"

"So, there is no final competition?"

"That is correct. You are all free to go home."

Cheers greeted his announcement and chairs scraped as they stood to leave. Wesley stood by the doorway and shook each contestant's hand, thanking them once again for everything and wishing them well.

"I can't believe it," Desiree said as she hugged Jodi.

"Me neither. But we need to keep in touch and maybe we can come back at the same time."

"Hey, you girls are hogging all the hugs." Tyler laughed as the rest of the group approached.

"Group hug!" Desiree shouted.

"And I think we should all come back at the same time. Right?" Jodi added.

"Right!"

☕

Jodi stood outside the Red Line Coffee Shop and smiled. It felt good to be home. The jingle of the bell over the door welcomed her.

Stevie was behind the counter, her back to the door. "Be right with you," she called out.

"No worries. I can take care of myself."

Stevie spun around. "You didn't have to come in today. I expected you to take a couple days off when you got home," Stevie pulled Jodi into a hug. "But tell me all about it."

Jodi pulled away. "I would have thought Jay had already done that."

"Pooh, he covered the basics, but I want to hear your side. How it affected all of you, and what the school is going to do."

Jodi laughed. "Pretty basic. I went, I competed, I made lifelong friends, and we all got a ten thousand dollar scholarship to the Whisper Peak Institute of Music. We can use it anytime, so we can still continue our current college studies. That's it."

"That's it?"

"What's it?" Leathers and Alexandria walked up.

"I just updated Stevie—"

"Wait, don't do it all again. This evening everyone will be here, and then you can update us all at once." Stevie hugged her again as she whispered, "Saved you."

Jodi whispered back, "You did. Thank you."

"Be here at closing with the others and we'll celebrate Jodi's home-coming and hear her story from beginning to end."

"From top to bottom," Jodi laughed and added, "And I expect a huge group hug from everyone!"

Meet the regular characters in the
Red Line Coffee Shop Mystery Series[1]

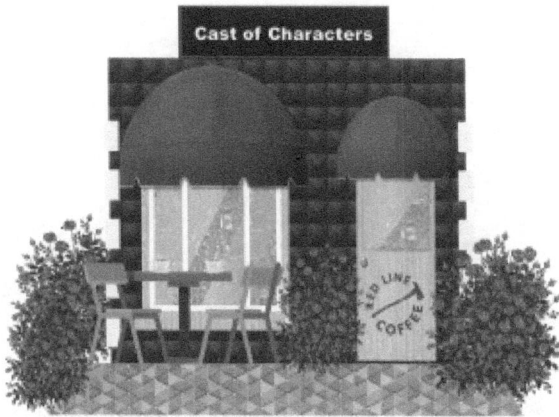

Owners of Red Line Coffee Shop
Garrett Phillips aka Flipper
Brett Davis aka Smokey
Stephanie (Stevie) Williams aka Grizz
Employees of Red Line Coffee Shop
Carl Jacobs aka Mugs - kitchen
Jodi Delgado aka Gabby - barista
Ray Dixon - barista
Townsfolk & Business Owners
Hank Maple - Mayor
Eldon Miller - Town Manager (Mayor's brother-in-law)
David Doughy aka Dough Boy - Chief of the Fire Department
Vita Corelli - Fire Department Admin (sister-in-law to the chief)
George Nikolaus aka Weezy - Retired Arson Investigator
Charles (Charlie) Hoye aka Newsie - Owner/Editor of *Jumpers Hole Gazette*

---

1. *https://books.dbmcnicol.com/rlc*

Marcie Grew - Admin to Newsie (and his daughter)
Ruby Karras - Owner of Ruby's Diner
Tom & Jerry Barbera - Brothers/Owners of the Drippy Cone Ice Cream Parlor
Carlo Forti - Head Baker & Owner of the Upper Crust Bakery
Jack Alldone - Coroner & Owner of Alldone Funeral Home

About the Author

Donna B. McNicol writes stories set in small-town, USA. Whether it's a tourist town, a town bypassed by the highway, or a Hawaiian island, the people drive her stories. Good or bad, friend or foe, they all have stories to tell. While her main genre is mysteries with a dash of romance, she has also tackled children's stories, fantasy, and small-town romance. In addition, her short stories have been included in several anthologies.

She has written while living full-time in an RV, on cruise ships, at local McDonald's restaurants, and from her rural current home in middle Tennessee where she resides with her husband and their two goofy Goldendoodles. You can sign up for her newsletter and be among the first to hear about new releases, discounts, sales & a lot more on her website! DBMcNicol.com

Read more at https://dbmcnicol.com/.

Made in United States
Cleveland, OH
29 April 2025